Other Books by Cheryl Campbell

Darling the Curly Tailed Reindoe

Darling Saves Christmas, The Continuing
Adventures of Darling the Curly Tailed Reindoe

Children can go to Darling's website at
www.reindoe.com to interact with Darling or Billy.

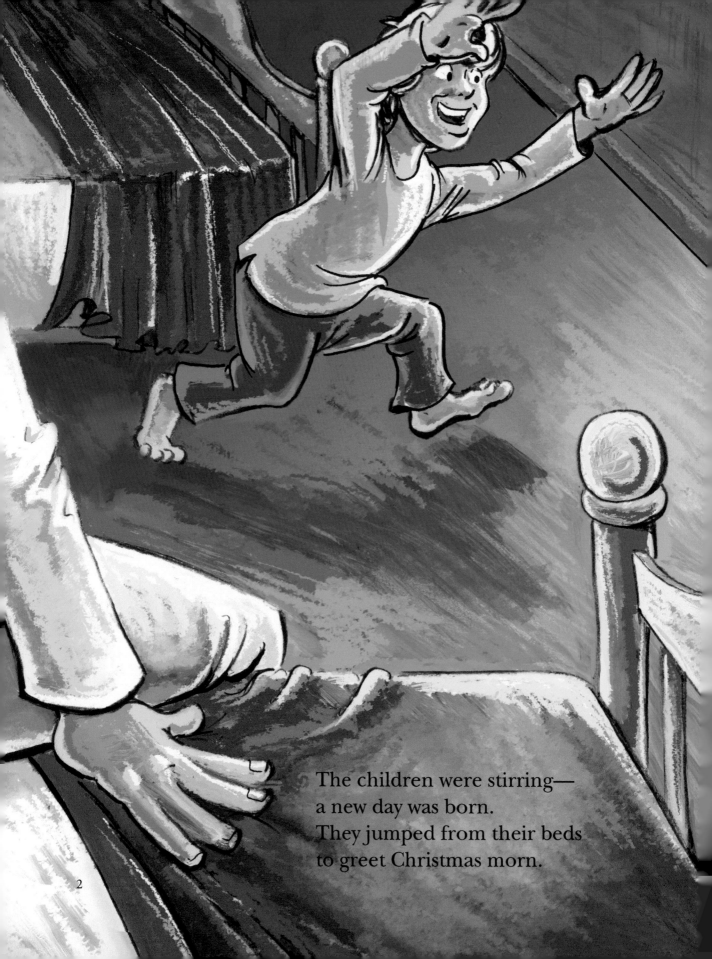

The children were stirring—
a new day was born.
They jumped from their beds
to greet Christmas morn.

2

Billy Mouse sleeping,
snug in his retreat,
was awakened by laughter
and pitter-pattering feet.

5

They ran to the window
and saw with delight—
it had started to snow
all during the night!

Billy crept to his doorway
with movements so slow
that he disturbed no one
while he peeked at the snow.

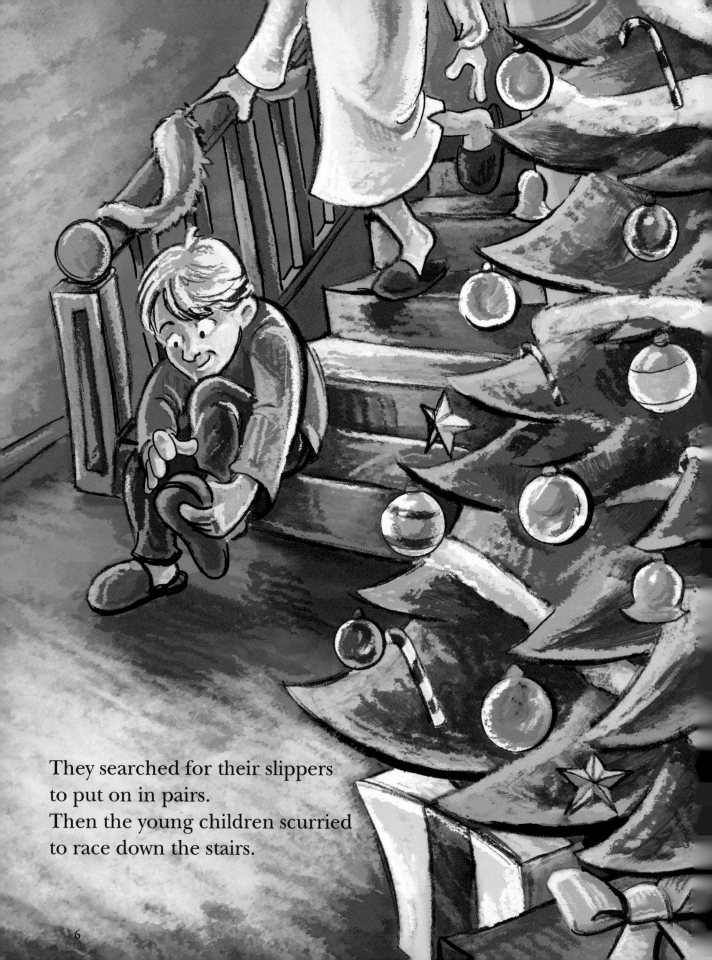

They searched for their slippers
to put on in pairs.
Then the young children scurried
to race down the stairs.

Billy snuck down behind them
and lo and behold,
the Christmas tree glittered
with silver and gold!

The children were laughing,
their joy growing more,
when they saw that their stockings
held presents galore.

8

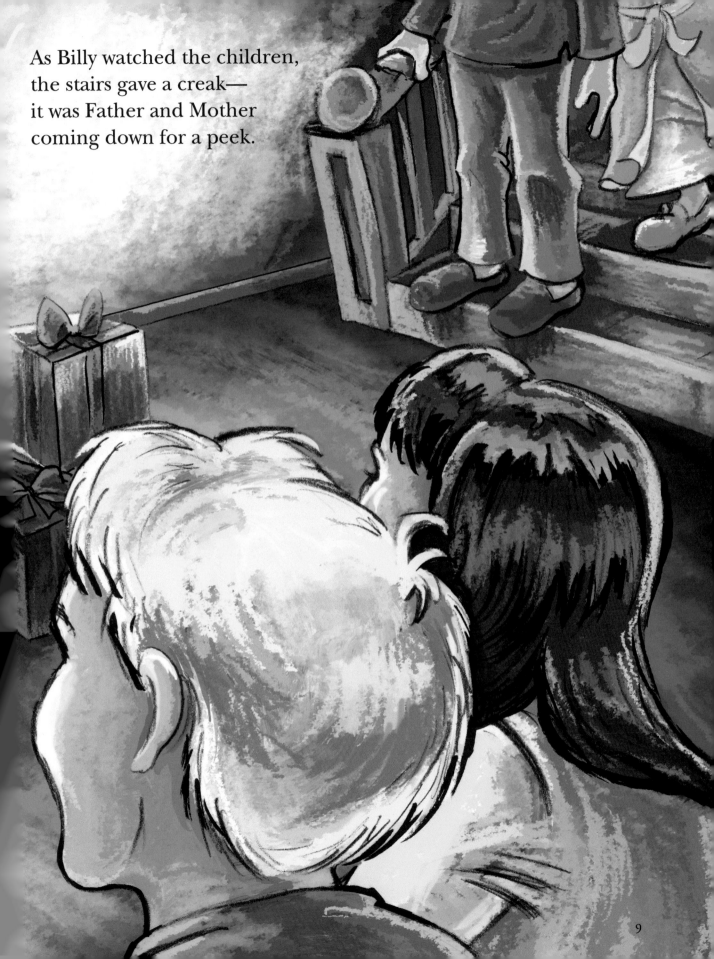

As Billy watched the children,
the stairs gave a creak—
it was Father and Mother
coming down for a peek.

9

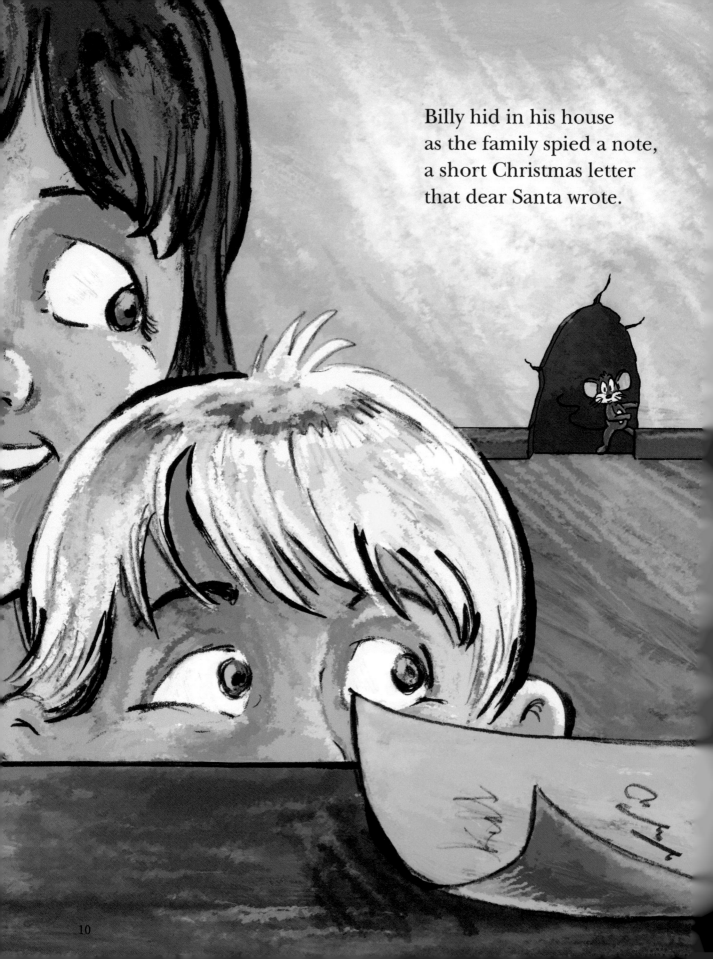

Billy hid in his house
as the family spied a note,
a short Christmas letter
that dear Santa wrote.

10

Father read the letter,
his voice soft and slow,
*The snack that you left me
was yummy. Ho! Ho! Ho!*

Billy crept to the mantle
where dear Santa's treat
had been on a special plate
filled with good things to eat.

Billy smiled and then sighed,
remembering the cheese,
how he had wanted to snatch some
as bold as you please.

Billy knew that Santa
would not miss a bite,
but he still didn't take one—
he did what was right.

Then Father finished reading,
My thanks one and all.
Your white Christmas snowflakes
will soon start to fall!

15

The children were smiling—
they'd just seen the snow,
like Santa had promised
when he wrote, *Ho! Ho! Ho!*

Mother and Father
shared their delight
as the snowflakes fell softly,
so delicate and white.

The gift wrap flew wildly,
and ribbons came free,
as they emptied their stockings
amid shouts of glee.

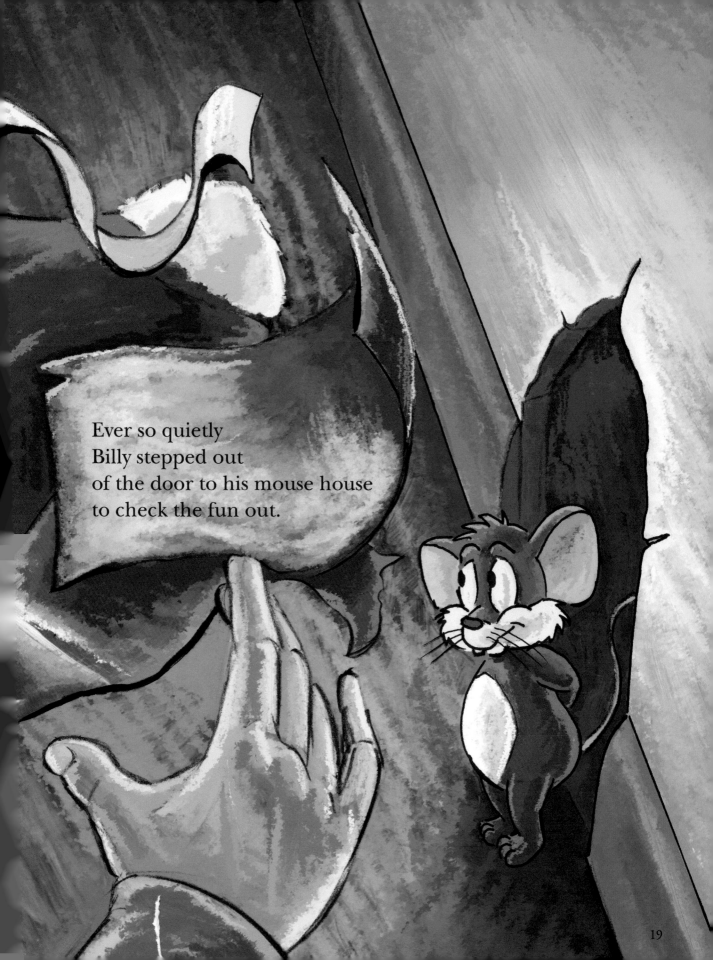

Ever so quietly
Billy stepped out
of the door to his mouse house
to check the fun out.

Surprise! He heard cheers
as he came into sight—
the family was laughing
with Christmas delight.

Billy ran quickly
so he too could see
the children so happy
and shouting with glee.

Then Father noticed
what others had missed
as they unwrapped the presents,
that huge pile of gifts!

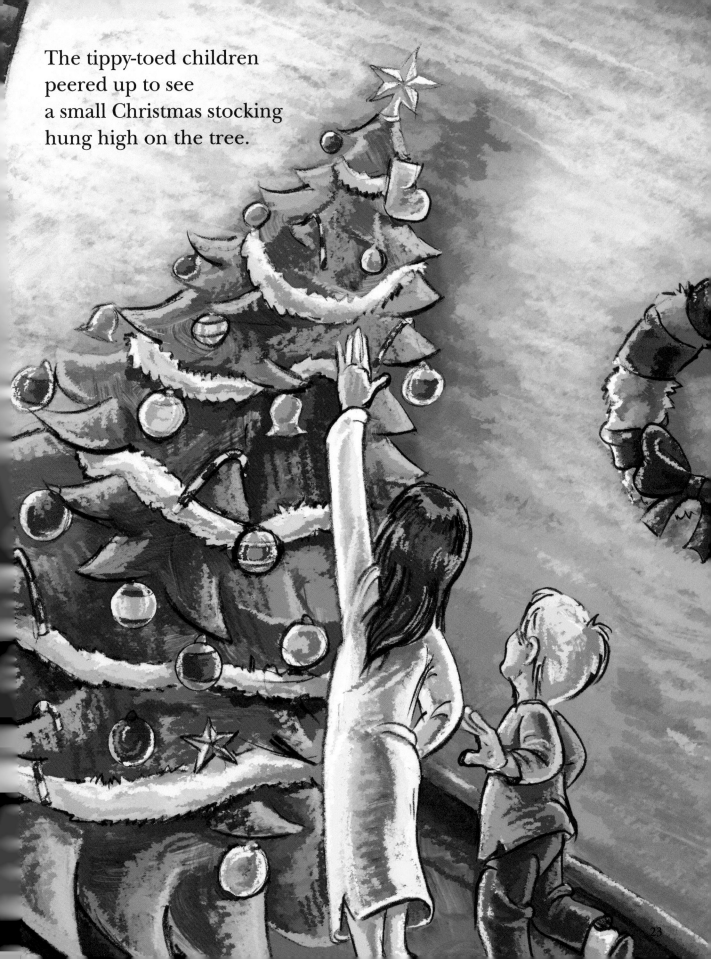

The tippy-toed children
peered up to see
a small Christmas stocking
hung high on the tree.

But Billy Mouse knew that
he'd been good all year.
Was the small stocking his?
Oh please, Santa dear!

He ran to the children
and thought, *Pretty please…*
his wish had been granted—
his stocking held cheese!

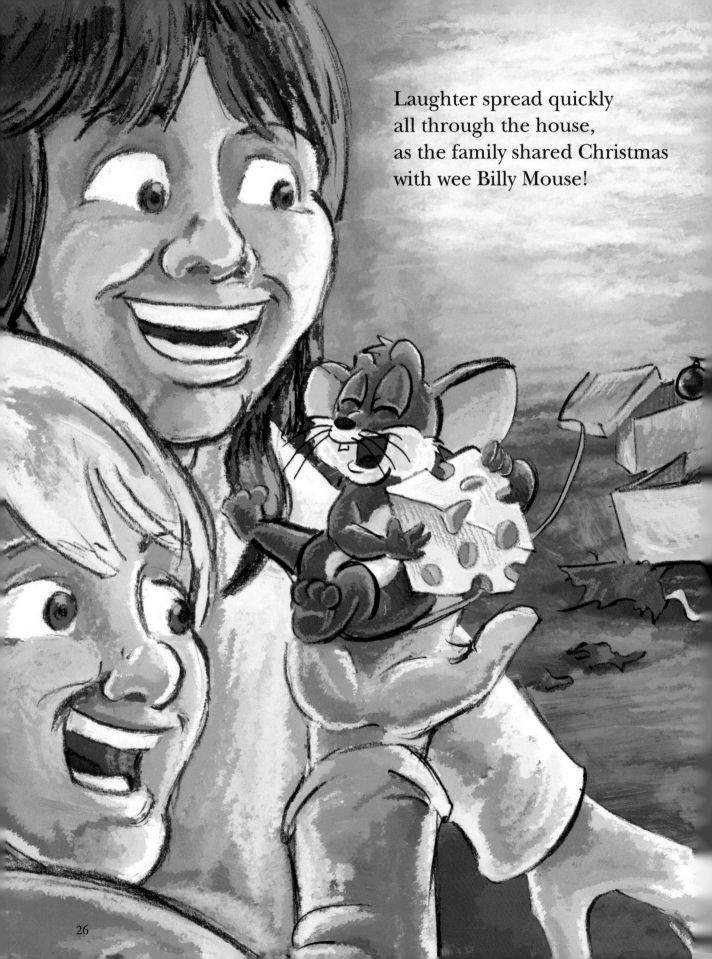

Laughter spread quickly
all through the house,
as the family shared Christmas
with wee Billy Mouse!